USBC PHOTOSHOTS

KINGS
AND
QUEENS

USBORNE HOTSHOTS

Kings
AND
Queens

Written by Philippa Wingate
Designed by Karen Tomlins

Illustrated by Peter Dennis, John Fox,
Ian Jackson, Colin King, Rodney Matthews,
Simon Roulstone, Sue Stitt and Ross Watton

Consultant: Dr. Anne Millard

Series editor: Judy Tatchell
Series designer: Ruth Russell

CONTENTS

4 Riches and regalia

6 A pharaoh's family

8 Royal warriors

10 The first and last emperors of China

12 Doomed monarchs

14 Golden empires

16 Mad, bad and dangerous

18 Powerful monarchs

20 Revolution!

22 Great builders

24 God kings

26 Elizabeth, past and present

28 Legendary kings

30 Royal gems

32 Index

Riches and regalia

A king, queen or emperor may be given a set of objects, called regalia, to symbolize their royal power. These objects are ornate and valuable.

Crowning glory

Most new rulers are presented with a crown at a ceremony called a coronation. Here are some crowns from around the world. Only the King Edward crown, shown on the right, is still in use.

The King Edward crown, used by monarchs of Great Britain and Northern Ireland.

The crown of the Holy Roman Empire, made for Otto I in the 10th century.

The Imperial Crown made for Catherine the Great of Russia (1729-96).

The Kiani crown, made in 1789 for Fath Ali, the Shah of Iran.

The crown of Reza, Shah of Iran, made in 1924.

The crown of Louis XVIII of France (1755-1824).

An Egyptian crown from around 2500BC.

A fly-whisk, part of the regalia of some African rulers.

Royal regalia

Here are some other sorts of regalia from different cultures and periods in history.

The ruler of the Akan in Africa carries a ceremonial sword.

Egyptian pharaohs carried a ceremonial crook.

4

Enthroned

Many monarchs have a special chair or stool, called a throne. The throne is usually placed on a mound or platform, to raise the monarch above the people. The picture on the right shows some of the world's most famous thrones, past and present.

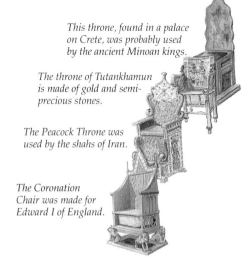

This throne, found in a palace on Crete, was probably used by the ancient Minoan kings.

The throne of Tutankhamun is made of gold and semi-precious stones.

The Peacock Throne was used by the shahs of Iran.

The Coronation Chair was made for Edward I of England.

First class travel

Monarchs travel around their kingdoms in great luxury. Here are some royal vehicles.

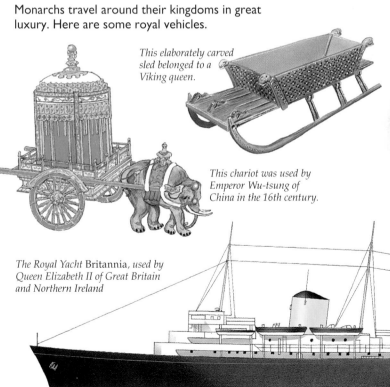

This elaborately carved sled belonged to a Viking queen.

This chariot was used by Emperor Wu-tsung of China in the 16th century.

The Royal Yacht Britannia, *used by Queen Elizabeth II of Great Britain and Northern Ireland*

A pharaoh's family

Akhenaten ruled Egypt in the 14th century BC. He was a strong leader, challenging the power of the priests by banning the worship of all gods except Aten, a sun god.

Queen Nefertiti

Nefertiti was Akhenaten's best-loved wife. The king thought so highly of her that he gave her a second, official name, Neferneferuaten. Normally only kings were allowed to take a second name.

This bust of Queen Nefertiti was made of painted stone.

The mystery of Smenkhkare

In the 14th year of his reign, Akhenaten declared a new co-ruler, called Smenkhkare. Historians are not sure who Smenkhkare was. The pharaoh gave this new co-ruler Nefertiti's special name, Neferneferuaten.

A recent theory suggests Smenkhkare could have been Nefertiti herself. Akhenaten believed his wife would never give birth to a son, so he married their eldest daughter, Meritaten, instead. To compensate Nefertiti, he may have made her a "king". The mysterious Smenkhkare disappeared at the time of Akhenaten's death.

This statue of Akhenaten gives him rounded, feminine hips. The reason why is unknown.

Akhenaten and Nefertiti on a balcony in their palace.

6

A pharaoh's treasure

In 1922, an archeologist named Carter found a previously undiscovered tomb. It belonged to Tutankhamun, Akhenaten's son.

Some of the treasure found in the tomb

Carter made a hole in the door and peered in. Inside were the fantastic riches of a royal Egyptian burial. It was the only pharaoh's tomb to survive 3,000 years unplundered by robbers.

A large pendant, called a pectoral

A pendant

Tutankhamun

Tutankhamun was not an important ruler. He died when he was only 18. But the discovery of his splendid tomb means that he is now Egypt's best-known king.

Tutankhamun's body was found inside four coffins.

Inside the royal tomb

This funeral mask is a portrait of the young king.

The outer coffins are made of wood covered with 22 carat gold and semiprecious stones.

Mummified body

This coffin is made of solid gold.

Royal warriors

In the past, it was the duty of most monarchs to lead their countries into battle. Some kings and queens became famous as outstanding warriors.

Alexander the Great

Alexander ruled Macedonia, north of Greece, in the 4th century BC. He proved that he was a skilful soldier while still a teenager. He was a genius at military tactics, beating his enemies in battles, sieges and surprise attacks.

Part of a mosaic showing Alexander the Great in battle

Conquering an empire

A catapult used by Alexander's army

In 334BC, Alexander set out on an expedition to conquer a vast empire. It was to take him over ten years. This map shows the route his army took.

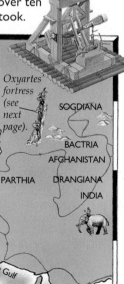

Black Sea

Caspian Sea

Oxyartes' fortress (see next page).

PERSIAN EMPIRE

SOGDIANA

BACTRIA

AFGHANISTAN

Mediterranean Sea

Tyre

Babylon

PARTHIA

DRANGIANA

INDIA

EGYPT

Red Sea

ARABIA

Persian Gulf

Alexander's adventures

In 334BC, Alexander invaded Persia and won four victories, despite being outnumbered.

Alexander defeating the Persians in battle

Alexander lay siege to Tyre, a city built on an island in the Mediterranean Sea. He floated out huge catapults to bombard the city, built a causeway and then captured the island.

In 328BC, Alexander came to King Oxyartes' fortress, which was built on a rock. Alexander's men drove iron pegs into the rock face. They attached rope ladders, climbed up and conquered the fortress.

When he reached India in 326BC, Alexander defeated King Porus, who gave him hundreds of elephants.

After ten years of fighting, the army refused to go on. They marched for home. Taken ill in Babylon, Alexander died in 323BC.

A warrior queen

Few military leaders successfully challenged the strength of the Romans. But Boudicca, queen of a British tribe called the Iceni, inflicted major defeats on their army.

In AD60, the Romans, who occupied much of Britain, seized the Iceni's land and flogged Boudicca in public.

Boudicca's revenge

Boudicca launched attacks on Roman settlements at Colchester, St. Albans and London. Her army burned the towns to the ground, killing 70,000 Romans.

Eventually, the Romans rallied their forces. They defeated Boudicca and her armies, killing 80,000 Iceni warriors. Queen Boudicca swallowed poison rather than be captured.

An Iceni war chariot

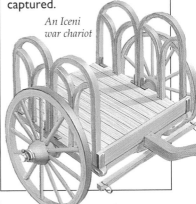

9

The first and last emperors of China

For over two thousand years, China was ruled by a succession of emperors. But the first and last emperors led very different lives.

Shih Huang Ti

The first man to unite the whole of China under his control was called Zheng. He was king of the province of Qin. In 221BC, he took the title Shih Huang Ti, which means "First Emperor".

Towers, built at regular intervals, housed 4-5 soldiers.

This map shows the extent of the Great Wall.

MONGOLIA

TIBET   The Great Wall

INDIA   CHINA

The Great Wall of China

During his reign, Shih Huang Ti built the largest man-made structure in the world. The Great Wall stretches 6,300km (4,000 miles) and can even be seen by astronauts orbiting the Earth.

The wall was built to keep out raiding tribes in the north, but some invaders bribed guards on the wall to let their armies into China.

The wall is up to 10m (32ft) high.

Slaves, prisoners and peasants were forced to work in terrible conditions to build the wall. Many thousands died.

10

A terracotta army

In 1974, farmers digging a well in Xian, China, came across a huge underground complex. They had found the tomb of the First Emperor.

The tomb is the largest ever discovered. Archeologists haven't excavated the burial chamber yet, but ancient records say that it is full of incredible riches.

Outside the chamber stands a life-size terracotta army of 7,500 soldiers, chariots and horses. They were put there to fight for the emperor in the Next World.

A terracotta soldier. Originally all the figures were brightly painted.

The terracotta army was found standing in long pits.

The last emperor of China

Pu Yi as a child

Pu Yi became emperor in 1908, at the age of two. His life began in great luxury, living in a palace known as the Forbidden City, in Beijing.

Revolution broke out in China when Pu Yi was only four years old. He was forced to give up his throne and leave the palace. The former emperor later spent five years in prison, before taking work as a gardener and a librarian.

The Forbidden City is the largest palace in the world. It has 8,000 rooms.

Doomed monarchs

European fortune hunters were responsible for the deaths of two 16th century monarchs in Mexico and Peru.

The last Aztec emperor

The Aztecs lived in Mexico from about 1325. In 1519, they were ruled by a man named Montezuma. In that year a group of Spanish adventurers, known as *conquistadors*, came searching for gold. They marched toward Tenochtitlán, the capital city. They were shown the way by a native woman who had fallen in love with Cortés, the Spanish leader.

An Aztec warrior   *A Spanish conquistador*

This temple was built on a huge mound of mud.

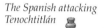
The Spanish attacking Tenochtitlán

The Aztecs had never seen horses and were terrified.

A portrait of Montezuma

Warrior gods

When the Spanish arrived in Tenochtitlán, the Aztecs were terrified of them. Some believed that Cortés was a god. But he seized and imprisoned Montezuma.

Cortés

When a rebellion broke out, Montezuma was sent out to try to calm his people. But he had always been an unpopular leader, and the crowd showered him with stones and arrows. The king died from his injuries.

12

A king's ransom

A similar fate awaited the ruler of the Incas of Peru. King Atahualpa was treated like a god. The gardens of his palace in the city of Cuzco were filled with plants and animals made of solid gold.

In 1533, a group of *conquistadors* came, led by a man named Pizzaro. They imprisoned the king and in return for his life, ordered the Incas to fill a room with gold. Today this ransom would have been worth the equivalent of about $170 million.

Even when the room was full of gold, Pizzaro refused to release the king. Atahualpa said farewell to his people before he was taken away and strangled to death by the Spanish. Pizzaro and his men then stole all the Inca gold.

This is an Inca city built high in a range of mountains in South America, called the Andes.

The Incas dug the mountain slopes into shelves and planted grain and vegetables.

Golden empires

Some kings are called emperors because they rule lands so huge that they hold power over other monarchs. Charlemagne and Kublai Khan ruled vast empires.

This picture shows Emperor Charlemagne on horseback.

Charlemagne

Charlemagne had a beautiful chapel built at Aachen, the capital city of his empire.

The Franks were a tribe that conquered a vast empire in Western Europe. The empire covered parts of modern France, Italy and Germany. It reached its greatest extent during the reign of Charlemagne, whose name means "Charles the Great". He came to power in AD768.

A golden bust of Charlemagne

Patron of the arts

Although Charlemagne himself never learned to read, he encouraged very high standards in learning, art, architecture and craftsmanship.

He founded schools and gathered some of Europe's greatest scholars at his court. Texts from the Bible and by classical authors were copied and sent to the libraries of monasteries.

The court of Kublai Khan

In the 13th century, a warrior tribe from northeast Asia, called the Mongols, conquered a vast empire covering land in China and the Middle East. From 1259, Kublai Khan was their emperor. He had a splendid court in Khanbalik (modern Beijing).

Kublai Khan wearing Chinese imperial robes

A map of the Mongol Empire

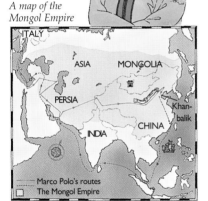

- - - Marco Polo's routes
- ☐ The Mongol Empire

Marco Polo

Many foreign merchants came to China to trade. Kublai Khan was so impressed by an Italian merchant named Marco Polo that he employed him as an ambassador for 17 years. When Polo returned home, a book was written about his adventures.

This is the first page of the book about Polo's travels.

New inventions

Kublai Khan ruled China at a time of fantastic inventions and discoveries, some of which are shown below.

The Chinese discovered how to make porcelain, a hard, fine type of china.

They used compasses to find their way across land and sea.

Paper money was used in China centuries before it was used in Europe.

The Chinese printed books with stamps like this one.

They invented gunpowder, which was first used in fireworks.

15

Mad, bad and dangerous

Henry VIII of England and Ivan IV of Russia are well known for their scandalous acts. The lives of both men were plagued by their need for heirs to their thrones.

Six wives for Henry

The lengths to which Henry VIII went to get a male heir shocked Europe. In 1509, he married Catherine of Aragon. But when all her sons died in infancy, Henry wanted the marriage declared invalid. The Pope refused, so Henry cut all ties between England and the Catholic Church in Rome.

Henry VIII, as painted by Hans Holbein

He then married Anne Boleyn. But when she failed to produce a son, he falsely accused her of being unfaithful to him and had her head cut off.

The king seemed genuinely fond of his third wife, Jane Seymour. But she died giving birth to a baby boy. The child was Henry's only male heir to survive infancy. His name was Edward and he was a weak, sickly child. He died at the age of 16 after reigning for only six years.

Henry divorced wife number four, Anne of Cleves, after only six months. At the age of 55, he fell in love with a teenager named Catherine Howard. But she was unfaithful to him and Henry had her put to death.

Henry's sixth wife, Catherine Parr, managed to escape the executioner's blade, because Henry died just before he could sentence her to death.

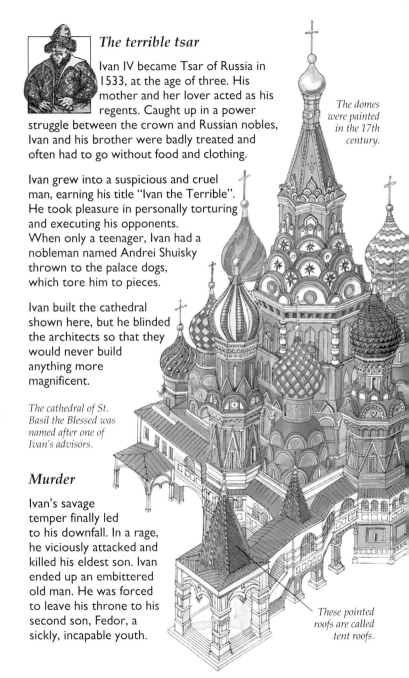

The terrible tsar

Ivan IV became Tsar of Russia in 1533, at the age of three. His mother and her lover acted as his regents. Caught up in a power struggle between the crown and Russian nobles, Ivan and his brother were badly treated and often had to go without food and clothing.

Ivan grew into a suspicious and cruel man, earning his title "Ivan the Terrible". He took pleasure in personally torturing and executing his opponents. When only a teenager, Ivan had a nobleman named Andrei Shuisky thrown to the palace dogs, which tore him to pieces.

Ivan built the cathedral shown here, but he blinded the architects so that they would never build anything more magnificent.

The cathedral of St. Basil the Blessed was named after one of Ivan's advisors.

The domes were painted in the 17th century.

Murder

Ivan's savage temper finally led to his downfall. In a rage, he viciously attacked and killed his eldest son. Ivan ended up an embittered old man. He was forced to leave his throne to his second son, Fedor, a sickly, incapable youth.

These pointed roofs are called tent roofs.

Powerful monarchs

In the 17th century, Louis XIV of France and Tsar Peter of Russia were famous for their power and wealth.

A mighty leader

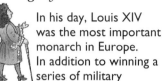

In his day, Louis XIV was the most important monarch in Europe. In addition to winning a series of military victories which extended France's boundaries, he was the cultural leader of Europe.

The Palace of Versailles

Louis' palace at Versailles became the model for palaces throughout the continent. It took 47 years to build and was renowned for its grandeur. Great crystal chandeliers hung from the ceilings, their candlelight reflected in gilded mirrors. Fine tapestries and paintings decorated the walls.

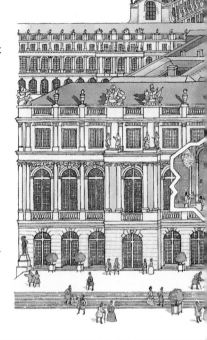

Peter the Great

In Russia, Tsar Peter (known as "Peter the Great") planned to transform his country into a great European power. He built up a strong, modern army and won victories against Sweden and Turkey. He introduced new industries and improved standards of education.

In his efforts to make Russia more modern, he forced the country's noblemen to cut off their old-fashioned beards.

The Great Palace, built by Peter outside St. Petersburg, was inspired by Versailles.

This picture shows the Palace of Versailles and some of its main rooms.

In this room, known as the Hall of Mirrors, one wall is covered with mirrors.

This emblem comes from the main gate of Louis' palace. It portrays Louis as the "Sun King".

Over 1,500 servants lived in the palace.

Fit for a king

Peter the Great even built himself a whole new city, and called it St. Petersburg. He wanted the city to be as great as any in Europe. He visited Germany, England and Holland, and employed the best artists, architects and craftsmen. The site for the city was wet and marshy ground at the mouth of a river named the Neva.

Forests had to be cleared, hills flattened and timbers driven into the marsh before building work could begin.

This picture shows part of the city of St. Petersburg.

Revolution!

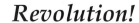

Many monarchs have been murdered by rivals or assassinated by madmen, but only a few have died in revolutions, at the hands of their own subjects.

Luxury and poverty

Soon after he inherited the throne of France in 1774, Louis XVI and his wife, Marie Antoinette, became hated for their extravagance and frivolity. They lived lives of great luxury, while many French people were starving.

Everything at court was very exaggerated, even the hairstyles.

Caught and executed

Unrest in France eventually led to the outbreak of revolution. Louis and his family attempted to flee the country, but they were caught, taken back to Paris and imprisoned.

The king was tried and executed in 1793, and his wife followed him to the guillotine only nine months later.

This sketch shows Marie Antoinette on the day of her execution.

Louis XVI and his wife were executed with a guillotine, like this one.

While a prisoner lay on a wooden bench, the blade was raised using the rope.

When the blade was released, it fell, cutting off the prisoner's head.

The prisoner placed his or her head here, between the two pieces of wood.

Executing the Romanovs

Tsar Nicholas Romanov II of Russia and his family enjoyed the wealth and luxury of life at court, until the Russian Revolution broke out in 1917.

These jewel-encrusted eggs were made for the tsar by a craftsman named Carl Fabergé.

The tsar was forced to give up his throne and the family was imprisoned in a town called Yekaterinburg.

On July 16, 1918, the revolutionaries began to fear the tsar might be rescued by his supporters. In the middle of the night, the Romanovs were awakened, taken down to a cellar and executed by a firing squad.

Their bodies remained unfound until 1991, when the bones of the tsar, his wife and three of their five children were discovered.

A photograph of the Romanov family

The missing princess

Shortly after the Romanovs disappeared, a young woman turned up in Berlin claiming to be Anastasia, the tsar's youngest daughter. She knew many details about Anastasia's life. She took the name Anna Anderson and spent 50 years trying to prove her story, until she died aged 82.

Her identity remained a mystery until 1994, when tests on her body tissue showed that she couldn't have been the tsar's daughter.

Anna Anderson

Great builders

Some monarchs are best remembered for the beautiful buildings that they commissioned during their reigns. Shah Jahan, Emperor of India and Ludwig II, King of Bavaria built great monuments to their dreams and desires.

Shah Jahan

Mumtaz Mahal

The chosen one

In 1612, Shah Jahan met his future wife while she was selling gifts in a bazaar. Their wedding was celebrated with great festivities and fireworks.

The shah gave his wife the name Mumtaz Mahal, which means "the Chosen One of the Palace". They were devoted to each other for 19 years, until Mumtaz died in childbirth.

A fitting monument

The grief-stricken shah decided to build a white marble tomb to match his wife's beauty. He called it the Taj Mahal.

Shah Jahan planned to build a second tomb for himself in black marble. But his plans were ruined when, in 1658, he was deposed by his son. He died in prison and was buried beside his wife.

The Taj Mahal

The shiny glaze on the white marble reflects the golden glow of the setting sun.

These are the public tombs of Shah Jahan and his wife.

They are actually buried here, in an underground chamber.

The Swan King

Ludwig II became the King of Bavaria (in Germany) in 1864. His subjects thought him a handsome, capable leader. In reality, he was a sad, lonely young man who behaved increasingly strangely.

Ludwig of Bavaria

Ludwig kept this life-size swan vase in his bathroom.

Ludwig was obsessed with fairy stories, particularly the tale of a Swan King. He spent vast sums of money building fantasy castles and palaces in which to live out his dreams.

His obsessions plunged Bavaria into debt. Ludwig's ministers had him removed from the throne and declared insane.

The castle of Neuschwanstein

A tragic end

In 1886, the king and his doctor were out walking in the grounds of Berg Castle. When they didn't return, a search party was organized. Their bodies were found in a lake.

Nobody knows if Ludwig's death was suicide or an accident. No water was found in his lungs, which suggests that he didn't drown.

God kings

Some cultures believed that their rulers were gods and goddesses living on Earth. They were thought to have special powers to control the weather or make crops grow.

A royal race

The ancient Egyptians believed that the position of pharaoh was introduced by the gods when the world was created. Pharaohs were descended from the great sun god Re, Egypt's first king.

They held special ceremonies with symbolic rituals to renew the pharaoh's power. Ramesses II (1304-1237BC) celebrated 14 of these ceremonies.

A bust of Ramesses II

Ramesses' renewal ceremonies

At a renewal ceremony, known as a *heb sed*, Ramesses would make offerings of food, wine, flowers and precious gifts to all the Egyptian gods and goddesses.

The pharaoh asked the gods to bless him with the strength and wisdom he needed to rule.

He had to perform a ceremonial run, to prove he was still fit and active enough to rule his country well.

After the run, Ramesses attended a ceremony at which priests crowned him pharaoh again.

The Dalai Lama

The political and religious ruler of Tibet is known as the Dalai Lama. The Tibetan people follow a religion called Buddhism and believe that the Dalai Lama's body contains the Buddhist spirit of compassion.

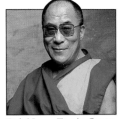

Dalai Lama Tenzin Gyatso

The Dalai Lama today

In 1951, Tibet was invaded by China. The fourteenth Dalai Lama, named Tenzin Gyatso, fled to India, where he lives in exile today.

The palace of Potala is the traditional residence of the Dalai Lamas.

The Red Palace

The White Palace

Some Buddhists believe the gods built Potala in one night.

Choosing a Dalai Lama

Tibetans believe that when a Dalai Lama dies, the spirit of compassion leaves his body and enters the body of a child born at exactly the same moment. The monks must find this child.

The dying Dalai Lama gives his monks information about where to find the new Dalai Lama.

The monks, who are known as "lamas" travel throughout Tibet looking for the special child.

There are tests to help them: one is that the baby recognizes the belongings of the previous Dalai Lama.

Elizabeth, past and present

The current queen of Great Britain and Northern Ireland is Elizabeth II. She has a famous predecessor, also named Elizabeth, who ruled England for nearly 50 years.

Elizabeth I

Elizabeth I came to the English throne in 1558. Her reign was outstandingly successful and her policies at home and abroad were very effective.

Elizabeth I

Elizabeth spoke five languages and loved riding, dancing and poetry. Once, a diplomat boasted that Elizabeth's rival, Mary Queen of Scots, was a fine musician. Elizabeth went straight to the virginals (a keyboard instrument) to prove that she could play brilliantly.

Elizabeth I was famous for her red hair and high hair line.

Following fashion

Many women at court copied the queen's appearance and style of dress. Elizabeth wore thick white makeup on her face. The lead in this makeup eventually destroyed her skin.

This portrait shows some of the fashions, such as large ruff collars, that Elizabeth inspired.

A modern queen

As a modern monarch, Queen Elizabeth II has a wide range of duties to perform. She is head of the armed forces, and all soldiers swear loyalty to her.

This picture is based on a state portrait of Her Majesty Queen Elizabeth II by Sir James Gunn.

The queen leads formal ceremonies. Below, she is going by carriage to the official opening of Parliament.

The queen makes foreign visits to encourage trade and help maintain friendly relations between Great Britain and other nations. Below, she is greeted by women in Jamaica.

Crowning a queen

These pictures show the stages of the coronation of Elizabeth II. Parts of the ceremony would have been the same for Elizabeth I.

The procession – the queen arrives at Westminster Abbey.

The recognition – the archbishop asks the people in the Abbey to accept the new monarch.

The oath – the queen swears to maintain laws and customs and to defend the Church.

The anointing – the archbishop uses holy oil to make the sign of a cross on the queen's body.

The crowning – the queen is dressed in robes and given the regalia. The archbishop places the crown on her head.

Legendary kings

Before writing was widely used, information about kings and queens was passed on by word of mouth. Gradually, weird and wonderful stories about ancient monarchs became legends.

A picture of Europa and Zeus from an ancient vase

King Minos of Crete

According to Greek legend, a god named Zeus fell in love with a princess, Europa. He changed himself into a bull and swam to the island of Crete with the princess on his back. One of Europa's sons, Minos, became King of Crete. He lived in a palace at Knossos. Today, experts think that "Minos" may have been a title, rather than the name of one man.

Mazes and monsters

Another legend tells of a prince who visited Crete. He killed a monster, half human and half bull, called the Minotaur. It lived in a maze called the Labyrinth. To later generations, the ruined palace at Knossos may have seemed like a maze, with its many rooms and corridors. Maybe the Minotaur was inspired by a Cretan king who wore a bull's head mask during religious ceremonies.

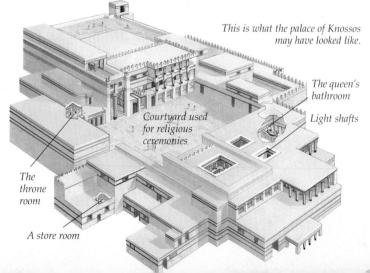

This is what the palace of Knossos may have looked like.

The queen's bathroom

Light shafts

Courtyard used for religious ceremonies

The throne room

A store room

King Arthur

Arthur was a legendary British king. There are many exciting stories about the adventures of Arthur and his band of knights. They lived in a palace called Camelot. Arthur himself is said to have inherited the throne because he was the only man able to remove a magical sword that had been plunged into a stone.

Arthur and his knights gathered at a round table.

Arthur's magical sword was named Excalibur.

King Arthur's name first appears in the ninth century writings of a monk named Nennius. Experts think that the real Arthur may have been a British war chief who led his people against Saxon invaders in about AD500.

Bones in the Abbey

In the twelfth century, monks living at the abbey in Glastonbury, England, claimed that they had uncovered the bones of King Arthur and his wife, Guinevere.

Nobody knows what the monks really found. They may have simply hoped to make money from pilgrims who would visit the abbey to see the bones of the legendary King Arthur.

Arthur holding Excalibur

Royal gems

There are many stories about monarchs and their historic deeds. Here are some of the more amazing tales.

Modern methods

In the 25th century BC, about 10,000 workers took 20 years to build a pyramid for King Khufu. In 1974, experts calculated that, with modern equipment, it would take 40 men just six years to complete.

An ambitious stepmother

In about 1500BC, Hatshepsut seized power from her stepson. As the statue of a god was

carried past her in a temple, it became so heavy that the priests carrying it sank to their knees. Insisting that this was a sign from the gods, Hatshepsut declared herself "King" of Egypt.

From slaughter to prayer

Asoka, King of the Mauryan empire in India, led his army to war in 273BC. Thousands of men were slaughtered. The sight of the dead and dying appalled the king so much that he became a Buddhist.

One of the many columns erected by King Asoka

Resting place

This picture shows the magnificent tomb of King Mausolus of Halicarnassus (now part of Turkey). The word mausoleum, meaning a building containing a tomb, comes from his name.

To the death

When the King of Siam died in 1424, his two eldest sons agreed to fight each other for the throne. They fought on the backs of elephants, and both were killed. Their younger brother became king instead.

Vlad the Impaler

Vlad was a 15th century prince of Wallachia (now part of Romania). He became infamous for impaling enemy soldiers and his own citizens on sharpened sticks. The legend of Dracula is based on Vlad.

Juana the Mad

Juana, heiress to the Spanish throne, refused to allow the burial of her dead husband. Declared unfit to govern, she was locked in a tower for 50 years, until her death in 1555.

A portrait of Juana

Brotherly love

When Mahomett III (1566-1603) ruled the Ottoman Empire he had all his brothers killed. He drowned seven pregnant ladies from the harem because their children would have been potential rivals.

Jinga the queen

Queen Jinga Mbandi personally negotiated the independence of her kingdom, Matamba, with a Portuguese governor. She sat on her servant because she wasn't offered a chair.

The Cage

In 17th century Turkey, the brothers of a new sultan were locked up in a group of rooms known as the "Cage". They were only released if they themselves were called upon to rule. Many sultans emerged from the Cage completely insane.

Sultan Osman II used human archery targets.

A tragic tale

Louis XIV's chef found he was short of lobsters for a sauce. He was so terrified of offending the king that he committed suicide.

Healing hands

Queen Anne

The English believed that victims of a skin disease, called scrofula, could be cured by the touch of a monarch's hand. The last British monarch asked to perform this treatment was Queen Anne (1665-1714).

A brief rule

The shortest reign was that of Crown Prince Filipe of Portugal, who was fatally wounded at the same time his father was shot dead in Lisbon in 1908. He was only king for about 20 minutes.

Big spender

In 1977, Jean Bedel Bokassa spent £20 million ($31 million) on his coronation as Emperor of the Central African Republic. At this time, the country's average wage was £16.50 (about $26) a year.

A detail from Bokassa's coronation robe

Fit for a sultan

The largest residential palace in the world belongs to the Sultan of Brunei. Completed in 1984, it cost about £300 million ($460 million) to build and has 1,788 rooms, 257 toilets and a garage that can hold over 110 cars.

Index

Akhenaten, Pharaoh of Egypt, 6-7

Alexander the Great, King of Macedonia, 8-9

Anastasia, 21

Anna Anderson, 21

Anne, Queen of England, 31

Atahualpa, King of the Incas, 13

Asoka, King of the Mauryan empire, 30

Aztecs, 12

Bokassa, Emperor of Central African Republic, 31

Boudicca, Queen of the Iceni, 9

Brunei, Sultan of, 31

Cage, the, 31

Camelot, 29

Charlemagne, King of the Franks, 14

conquistadors, 12, 13

coronation 4, 27

Cortés, Hernando, 12

Dalai Lama, 25

Elizabeth I, Queen of England, 26

Elizabeth II, Queen of Great Britain and Northern Ireland, 27

Europa, 28

Excalibur, 29

Fabergé, Carl, 21

Filipe, Prince of Portugal, 31

Forbidden City, 11

Franks, 14

Great Wall, 10

guillotine, 20

Guinevere, 29

Hatshepsut, Queen of Egypt, 30

heb sed, 24

Henry VIII, King of England, 16

Incas, 13

Ivan the Terrible, Tsar of Russia, 17

Jinga Mbandi, 31

Juana the Mad, 30

Khufu, King of Egypt, 30

Knossos, Palace of, 28

Kublai Khan, King of the Mongols, 15

Louis XIV, King of France, 18-19, 31

Louis XVI, King of France, 20

Ludwig II, King of Bavaria, 23

Mahomet III, Sultan of the Ottoman Empire, 31

Marie Antoinette, 20

Mausolus, King of Halicarnassus, 30

Minos, King of Crete, 28

Mongols, 15

Montezuma, Emperor of Aztecs, 12

Mumtaz Mahal, 22

Nefertiti, co-ruler of Egypt, 6

Neuschwanstein castle, 23

Nicholas II, Tsar of Russia, 21

Peter the Great, Tsar of Russia, 18-19

Pizzaro, 13

Polo, Marco, 15

Potala, palace of 25

Pu Yi, Emperor of China, 11

Ramesses II, Pharaoh of Egypt, 24

regalia, 4-5

Romanovs, 21

Shah Jahan, 22

Shih Huang Ti, Emperor of China, 10-11

Siam, King of, 30

St. Petersburg, 18-19

Taj Mahal, 22

Tenzin Gyatso, 25

thrones, 5

travel, 5

Tutankhamun, Pharaoh of Egypt, 7

Versailles, Palace of, 18-19

Vlad (the Impaler), Prince of Wallachia, 30

This book is based on material previously published in: *The Usborne Book of Kings and Queens; Early Civilizations; Who Built the Pyramids?; The Greeks; The Usborne Book of Explorers; Castles, Pyramids and Palaces; Tales of King Arthur.*

First published in 1996 by Usborne Publishing Ltd, Usborne House, 83-85 Saffron Hill, London EC1N 8RT, England.
Copyright © Usborne Publishing Ltd, 1996, 1995, 1991, 1990, 1989
The name Usborne and the device ⊕ are Trade Marks of Usborne Publishing Ltd.
All rights reserved. No part of this publication may be reproduced, stored in a retrieval system or transmitted in any form or by any means, electronic, mechanical, photocopying, recording or otherwise, without the prior permission of the publisher.
First published in America August 1996 UE
Printed in Italy.

The publisher would like to thank the following organizations for permission to reproduce their material: The Mansell Collection, London, page 11; Popperfoto, page 21; Hulton Deutsch page 21, 23, The Office of Tibet, London, page 25; Press Association, page 31